by Lyle Spencer

SCHOLASTIC INC.
New York   Toronto   London   Auckland   Sydney
Mexico City   New Delhi   Hong Kong   Buenos Aires

PHOTO CREDITS
NBA Entertainment Photos
Cover: Andrew D. Bernstein. 4, 5, 6, 11, 14, 20, 28, 33, 34, 35, 36, 37: Andrew D. Bernstein. 13, 18: NBA Photo Library. 19, 21, 23, 27: Nathaniel S. Butler. 24: Andy Hayt. 38: Robert Mora.

9: Special thanks to Lucille Harrison.

ISBN 0-439-35184-7

12 11 10 9 8 7 6 5 4 3 2 1   2 3 4 5 6 7/0

Printed in the U.S.A.
First Scholastic printing, February 2002
Book Design: Louise Bova

Contents

A Champion On and Off the Court

Shaquille O'Neal is a champion in life. He cares about all people, but he especially loves children. That's because Shaq still thinks of himself as a big kid.

Everyone seems small next to Shaq, even his teammates. That's because Shaq is seven feet,

Kobe Bryant and Shaq

one inch tall and weighs 315 pounds. But the biggest thing about Shaq is not his height or his muscles. It is his heart. He has helped thousands of people with charities and gifts. On Thanksgiving Day every year, Shaq hands out free turkeys to people who cannot afford them.

On the basketball court, Shaq is not quite as nice if you play for the other team. He gives everything he has to win. He plays with all of his heart and energy to help the Los Angeles Lakers win. They have won back-to-back NBA championships. Shaq wants his team to win a third time this year.

Winning championships makes Shaq feel great. But it's more important to him that all the other teams tried their best. Shaq says there are no losers in the

NBA. He worries that people care too much about winning. Shaq wants everyone to have fun and enjoy the game.

Shaq at the L.A. Lakers Championship parade

Shaq has been named the Most Valuable Player in the league and in the playoffs twice. He has also been Most Valuable Player of the All-Star Game. He was named one of the 50 Greatest Players in NBA history. Shaq knows that he is lucky. He feels blessed that he is able to do something he enjoys and give pleasure to so many people.

Winning two championships with the L.A. Lakers made Shaq very happy. The best part was sharing the joy with his teammates and coaches. Shaq loved the parade after the Lakers won their second straight championship. Half a million people came to cheer, including thousands of children. Shaq sang and danced. It was a big party. Shaq never has been happier, because he was born to entertain. Nothing gives him more pleasure.

Growing Up . . . and Up

Shaquille Rashaun O'Neal was born on March 6, 1972, in Newark, New Jersey. His mother, Lucille, picked his name out of a book. Shaquille Rashaun means "little warrior" in Arabic. Shaq has two younger sisters, Ayesha and Lateefah, and a little brother, Jamal.

Shaq's mom did not know her first child would grow to be so big. He was 7 pounds, 11 ounces at birth. Shaq grew so quickly, nobody would believe he was his age. His mother had to carry his birth certificate so Shaq could get the child's fare on the train in New Jersey.

Because Shaq's dad, Philip, was an Army sergeant, his family moved around a lot when Shaq was young. After New Jersey, Shaq lived in Germany and then in Georgia. Shaq's father was

Baby Shaq, age 1

very strict. When Shaq didn't do his homework or got into fights with kids who were making fun of his size, he knew he was going to get in trouble from his dad.

Football was Shaq's favorite sport as a kid, but he was afraid of the ball. His dad taught him to get over his fear. Shaq became a good football player. But he got hit hard in the knees one time and decided that basketball was better suited for him.

SHAQ'S GROWTH CHART

Age 4: 3-10 ½, 56 pounds
Age 6: 4-4, 82 pounds, size 2 shoe
Age 10: 5-3, 139 pounds, size 7 ½ shoe
Age 12: 5-10, 192 pounds, size 10½ shoe
Age 16: 6-8, 265 pounds, size 15 shoe
Age 21: 7-1, 302 pounds, size 20 shoe
Age 25: 7-1, 310 pounds, size 22 shoe
Age 29: 7-1, 315 pounds, size 22 shoe

Shaq's dad had been a basketball player in junior college and taught Shaq how to pass, shoot and dribble. Shaq went to a game in New York with his dad and watched his favorite player, Julius Erving, which got him excited about the game. Shaq

Shaq and his hero, Superman

worked hard on his basketball skills but was not very good at first. He did not make the team in his first year of high school. But he kept practicing and kept getting better.

Shaq was living on an army base in Germany when he met a man named Dale Brown. He was the coach at Louisiana State University. Coach Brown thought Shaq was one of the soldiers living on the base. Shaq was only 15 years old, but he was already six-foot-eight! Coach Brown always remembered Shaq and helped him start his basketball career.

When Shaq's family moved to San Antonio, Texas, Shaq went to Cole High School. He made the basketball team and became one of the best players in the country. His team won the state championship.

Coach Brown kept in touch with Shaq during high school and asked him to come to Louisiana State University on a scholarship. Shaq had many offers to go to other universities, but he remembered meeting Coach Brown in Germany. Coach Brown also reminded Shaq of his father because he was very strict.

Shaq made a decision very quickly. He was moving to Louisiana to play for Coach Brown.

College Life

Shaq was excited to leave his home in San Antonio to go to Louisiana State University. He was happy that he would be playing for Coach Dale Brown. Shaq was sure Coach Brown would discipline him in order to make him as good as he could be, just like his dad had always done.

But Shaq also knew he would have to study just as hard as he practiced basketball. He made a promise to his mother that he would graduate from college. Nothing was more important to Shaq than his word to his mother.

Things were not easy for Shaq at LSU. He quickly learned that there were players much closer to his size playing college ball. One was a teammate, Stanley Roberts. Stanley was also a

Shaq loves to relax at home.

seven-foot center with a lot of muscle. Shaq learned a lot playing against Stanley in practice.

Shaq also watched NBA players closely. He studied the moves of David Robinson, Patrick Ewing and Rony Seikaly. Coach Brown gave Shaq keys to the gym at LSU. Every day he tried

to learn the moves that had made his heroes successful NBA centers.

Shaq was not the best player at LSU as a fresh-man. Stanley Roberts and Chris Jackson, a spectacu-lar little guard, did most of the scoring. Shaq was happy to rebound and play mostly defense. His big scoring days came the next year. As a sophomore, Shaq averaged 27.6

points and 14.7 rebounds per game. He was well known by basketball fans all around the country.

Shaq met two NBA superstars during his sophomore year. Kareem Abdul-Jabbar and Bill Walton visited LSU's campus to teach Shaq moves and talk to him about the game. Shaq was amazed that these famous players knew who he was and wanted to help him. All of his hard work was paying off.

During his junior year, Shaq got a big surprise. His childhood hero, Julius "Dr. J" Erving, came to visit him. Dr. J talked to Shaq about the importance of being a good role model for young people. Dr. J had earned a degree from the University of Massachusetts and had become a big success both on and off the court. That left a huge impression on Shaq.

Wilt Chamberlain, another former NBA superstar, watched Shaq play and was very impressed. He said Shaq reminded him of himself when he was younger. Shaq took that as a big compliment. Wilt was the most famous center of his time. He was a great scorer and rebounder who once scored 100 points in an NBA game!

By his junior year, Shaq was known as the best college player in America. He averaged 24.1 points and 14 rebounds per game even though he was always guarded with two or three players. That was a great year for Shaq. But he was frustrated when his team didn't win the NCAA Tournament.

Shaq did everything he could to help his team win. He made dunks and jump shots and made all 12 of his free throw attempts. He scored 36 points. He also blocked five shots. But LSU lost the game to Indiana, 89–79. Shaq cried in the locker room after the game. Even though Shaq was a junior, this was his last college game. He knew he was ready for the NBA.

Magic Kingdom

It was no surprise when the Orlando Magic chose Shaq as the first pick in the 1992 NBA Draft. Everyone knew he was great. Players like Shaq come along once in a generation.

Before he moved to Orlando, Florida, Shaq went to Los Angeles to spend some time with Magic Johnson. The Lakers' superstar gave Shaq a lot of advice. They played basketball together and Magic taught Shaq some new tricks.

Shaq went on to have a great first season in Orlando.

The Magic won 20 more games than they had the season before. Shaq was named NBA Rookie of the Year. He averaged 23.4 points and 13.9 rebounds per game. He played in his first All-Star Game and scored 14 points.

After his first season in Orlando, Shaq went back to Los Angeles. He made a shoe commercial and filmed a movie about basketball called *Blue Chips*. Shaq started making music, too. He was recording rap songs that would become big hits. And he was still only 21 years old.

Shaq's second season was even better than his first. He raised his scoring to 29.3 points per game. He had the best

Shaq has made six rap albums!

shooting percentage in the NBA. He made 6 out of every 10 shots! Shaq also got to play in another All-Star Game. The best part of all was that Orlando made the playoffs for the first time ever!

In his third season, Shaq led the NBA in scoring, with 2,315 total points and 29.3 points per game. Orlando won 57 games and won the Atlantic Division. The Magic made it all the way to the NBA Finals. Even though Houston won the championship, Shaq made a big impression on their superstar, Hakeem Olajuwon. Olajuwon said that Shaq would win championships someday.

Shaq was injured in the 1995–96 season. He missed

28 games. He still had a good season, but not as good as he had hoped. He played well in the All-Star Game again. The Magic won 60 games and the Atlantic Division again. But they lost to Chicago in the playoffs. Shaq started to think that maybe it was time for a change.

By now, Shaq was interested in many things besides basketball. He'd started making rap CDs and was very successful. He also was interested in making more movies.

Most important, he was taking classes. He wanted to graduate from college at LSU. He had not forgotten his promise to his mother.

That summer, Shaq was named to the United States Olympic team. He played in the 1996 Summer Games in Atlanta. He helped the United States win a gold medal in the Olympics. Shaq was very proud when they put the gold medal around his neck.

Right before the Olympics began, Shaq made

a big announcement. It shook up the NBA like one of Shaq's biggest dunks. He was moving again — to Los Angeles. Shaq wanted to be a Laker.

Shaq practices with Kobe Bryant.

Go West, Young Man

Shaq had always dreamed of playing for the Lakers. He was a big fan of Magic Johnson. Getting to know Magic in 1992 had been a thrill for Shaq. Now Magic was one of the owners of the Lakers. Jerry West, another great Laker from the past, was in charge of the team.

Shaq was sad to leave behind Dennis Scott and Horace Grant and other good friends with the Magic. But he knew he'd always make new friends. Because he had moved from one military base to another when he was young, Shaq knew that it was fun to have new experiences.

Kobe Bryant started playing for Los Angeles at the same time as Shaq. Kobe was only 18 years old. He had great talent but there was a lot he needed to learn. The Lakers had other excellent players, but they needed time to grow as a team.

Shaq's first season in Los Angeles was frustrating. He missed 31 games with injuries, but he recovered in time for the playoffs. Shaq gave everything he had in the playoffs. The Lakers beat Portland in their first series, but then lost to Utah, ending the season.

His second season with the Lakers was a lot like the first. Shaq missed 21 games because of injuries. But he still finished second in scoring. That year he played in his fifth All-Star Game. Shaq was healthy for the playoffs. He led the Lakers to series wins over both Portland and Seattle. But the Lakers lost to Utah again in the conference finals.

In 1999, Shaq worked hard to get the Lakers into the playoffs. They beat Houston in the first series but lost to San Antonio in the second series. Shaq started to wonder how they could win an NBA championship.

After the 1998–99 season, the Lakers hired Phil Jackson as head coach. Jackson had coached Chicago to six championships with Michael Jordan. Shaq visited his new coach's home in Montana. Jackson reminded Shaq of his father. He was very strong-willed and Shaq knew

Shaq rests with Kobe during a game.

Shaq gives Kobe a free ride.

he would inspire the Lakers.

Coach Jackson made a big difference. The Lakers were the best team in the NBA in 1999–2000. The team had Ron

Harper, A.C. Green, Glen Rice, Robert Horry, Brian Shaw and Rick Fox. They were older players with a lot of experience. Shaw had played with Shaq in Orlando. Shaq was happy to have his old friend with him again.

Shaq was voted league Most Valuable Player for the first time. He also was MVP of the All-Star Game, along with Tim Duncan. Shaq won his second scoring title. He averaged 29.7 points per game.

In the playoffs, the Lakers beat Sacramento, Phoenix and Portland to reach the Finals. Shaq was at his best. He scored 43, 40, 33, 36, 35 and 41 points in the six games against Indiana.

MAJOR AWARDS

- Olympic gold medal, 1996, Atlanta Summer Games
- NBA Champion, 2000 and 2001
- NBA Most Valuable Player, 2000
- NBA Finals Most Valuable Player, 2000 and 2001
- One of the 50 Greatest Players in NBA History, 1996
- First team All-NBA, 1998, 2000, 2001
- Eight-time NBA All-Star (1992–2001)
- All-Star Game MVP, 2000
  (Co-All-Star Game MVP with Tim Duncan)
- NBA Rookie of the Year, 1993
- Gold medal, U.S. World Championship team, 1994, World Championships in Toronto

He was the Finals MVP. The Lakers had won their first championship since 1988!

Shaq cried on the STAPLES Center court after winning the championship. His mom and dad were hugging him. His teammates all said he was the greatest. He finally knew what it felt like to be an NBA champion.

Shaq liked winning so much that he decided to do it again. The Lakers were almost perfect in the 2001

playoffs. They won every game against Portland, Sacramento and San Antonio. Eleven wins in a row. Then they lost in Game 1 of the Finals against Philadelphia. But they won the next four games and were crowned champions again. Shaq once again was the Finals MVP.

All of Shaq's dreams had come true. He was a two-time NBA champion with the Lakers. He had everyone's respect now. He was not just the biggest. He was the best.

Real-Life Superman

Shaq is as big as two people — inside and out. There is fierce, powerful Shaq, king of the court. And there is gentle, generous, happy-go-lucky Shaq, that his family and friends know best.

Shaq's favorite comic book hero as a kid was Superman. Shaq's homes in Florida and California are full of Superman logos. Shaq loves Superman because he always helps people in trouble. Shaq tries to be as kind and generous as Superman is.

On Christmas Day, he dresses up as "Shaq-a-Claus" and takes presents to needy children. On Thanksgiving, he delivers dozens of turkeys (Shaqsgiving). Shaq contributed a million dollars to the Boys & Girls Clubs of America to start technology centers. He loves computers and

wanted to be sure that kids across America have a chance to use them. He has asked successful businesspeople such as Bill Gates to help with his programs. They have helped him raise millions of dollars for charities. Shaq is also a spokesman for

Reading Is Fundamental, because he understands the importance of learning to read.

On December 15, 2000, Shaq made good on his promise to his mother. He graduated from Louisiana State University. He even missed a

Shaq's house!

game to attend his graduation! The Lakers were happy to see him do it. They knew how much it meant to Shaq. He had been taking courses for a long time to get his degree.

Shaq also has his own record company. It is

Shaq graduated from LSU on December 15, 2000

called T.W.I.S.M. Records. One of Shaq's albums, *Shaq Diesel*, sold more than one million copies. Two others sold more than 200,000 copies apiece. He modeled his rap style after two of his favorite rappers, Run DMC and LL Cool J.

Shaq loves movies of all kinds. He has starred in *Blue Chips*, *Kazaam* and *Steel*. He enjoys meeting the famous actors and actresses who attend Lakers games. He is friends with Denzel Washington and Jack Nicholson, who come to most of the games. He has met Janet Jackson, Madonna, Tyra Banks and many other stars.

When Shaq has time off on the road during the season, he can often be found at the local zoo. He loves the big animals and the primates. He likes watching the animals and laughing with all the kids who come to the zoo. He poses for photos with children and signs autographs.

In his free time, Shaq loves to play video

games. He even has a game room in his house! His very own arcade, he calls it. He has a pool table and a Pepsi machine. Shaq could spend hours going from game to game. He also enjoys water sports. He rides a Jet Ski on the lake outside his home in Florida. He has fun riding go-karts — if they can find one big enough for him. He also likes to wrestle with buddies when they come to visit him.

Shaq also likes to drive around Los Angeles. He has many different cars to suit his different moods. He also loves to ride his custom-made Harley-Davidson motorcycle. He likes to put on his helmet and ride his big bike through the streets of Los Angeles. He smiles and waves when people shout, "Hey, it's Shaq!"

Everyone who meets Shaquille O'Neal loves him — because he is a true champion. And Shaq plans to be one for a long time.

Shaq Facts...

ALL-TIME NBA REGULAR SEASON SCORING LEADERS:

1. Michael Jordan   31.5
2. Wilt Chamberlain   30.1
3. SHAQUILLE O'NEAL   27.7
4. Elgin Baylor   27.4
5. Jerry West   27.0

ALL-TIME PLAYOFF SCORING LEADERS:

1. Michael Jordan   33.4
2. Jerry West   29.1
3. SHAQUILLE O'NEAL   28.2
4. Elgin Baylor   27.0
5. George Gervin   27.0

SHAQ'S CAREER BESTS:

Points: 61 (3/00 vs. Clippers)
Field goals made: 24 (3/00 vs. Clippers)
Field goals attempted: 40 (3/96 vs. Washington)
Free throws made: 19 (11/99 vs. Chicago)
Free throws attempted: 31 (11/99 vs. Chicago)
Rebounds: 28 (11/93 vs. New Jersey)
Assists: 9 (twice)
Steals: 5 (three times)
Blocked shots: 15 (11/93 vs. New Jersey)